CELEBRITY
CELIA

Level 5F

Written by Louise Goodman
Illustrated by Kimberley Scott
Reading Consultant: Betty Franchi

About Phonics

Spoken English uses more than 40 speech sounds. Each sound is called a *phoneme*. Some phonemes relate to a single letter (d-o-g) and others to combinations of letters (sh-ar-p). When a phoneme is written down, it is called a *grapheme*. Teaching these sounds, matching them to their written form, and sounding out words for reading is the basis of phonics.

Early phonics instruction gives children the tools to sound out, blend, and say the words without having to rely on memory or guesswork. This instruction gives children the confidence and ability to read unfamiliar words, helping them progress toward independent reading.

About the Consultant

Betty Franchi is an American educator with a Bachelor's Degree in Elementary and Middle Education as well as a Master's Degree in Special Education. Betty holds a National Boards for Professional Teaching Standards certification. Throughout her 24 years as a teacher, she has studied and developed an expertise in Phonetic Awareness and has implemented phonetic strategies, teaching many young children to read, including students with special needs.

Reading tips

This book focuses on the *s* sound (made with the letter *c* when followed by *e*, *i*, or *y*) as in **ce**nt, **ci**rcus, and **cy**st.

Tricky and/or new words in this book

Any words in bold may have unusual spellings or are new and have not yet been introduced.

> **Tricky and/or new words in this book**
>
> ## wants being who
> ## physicist please come

Extra ways to have fun with this book

After the readers have read the story, ask them questions about what they have just read.

What did Celia do on the stage?
Celia's parents say she can stay on the stage as long as she does what?

You're looking for the theatre? I wish I could point you in the right direction.

THEATRE

A Pronunciation Guide

This grid contains the sounds used in the stories in levels 4, 5, and 6 and a guide on how to say them.

/ă/ as in pat	/ā/ as in pay	/âr/ as in care	/ä/ as in father
/b/ as in bib	/ch/ as in church	/d/ as in deed/ milled	/ĕ/ as in pet
/ē/ as in bee	/f/ as in fife/ phase/ rough	/g/ as in gag	/h/ as in hat
/hw/ as in which	/ĭ/ as in pit	/ī/ as in pie/ by	/îr/ as in pier
/j/ as in judge	/k/ as in kick/ cat/ pique	/l/ as in lid/ needle (nēd'l)	/m/ as in mom
/n/ as in no/ sudden (sŭd'n)	/ng/ as in thing	/ŏ/ as in pot	/ō/ as in toe
/ô/ as in caught/ paw/ for/ horrid/ hoarse	/oi/ as in noise	/ʊ/ as in took	/ū/ as in cute

/ou/ as in out	/p/ as in pop	/r/ as in roar	/s/ as in sauce
/sh/ as in ship/ dish	/t/ as in tight/ stopp**ed**	/th/ as in thin	/th/ as in this
/ŭ/ as in cut	/ûr/ as in urge/ term/ firm/ word/ heard	/v/ as in valve	/w/ as in with
/y/ as in yes	/z/ as in zebra/ xylem	/zh/ as in vision/ pleasure/ garage/	/ə/ as in about/ item/ edible/ gallop/ circus
/ər/ as in butter			

Be careful not to add an /uh/ sound to /s/, /t/, /p/, /c/, /h/, /r/, /m/, /d/, /g/, /l/, /f/ and /b/. For example, say /fff/ not /fuh/ and /sss/ not /suh/.

Celia **wants** to be a celebrity on the stage.

She imagines **being** a star by riding a unicycle, playing the cymbals, and ice skating.

Celia's parents, **who** are both professors, want her to be a **physicist**. One day, Celia packs a bag and sets off for the theatre.

Celia begs the director to let her in the show. "Oh **please**, please," she cries.

"Hush!" says the director.
"I don't want any stress.
We'll give you a try."

Celia learns to ride a unicycle,

clash the cymbals,
and skate on the ice.

Celia is soon the star of the show.

Every night she performs more
and more amazing tricks.

She plays the cymbals
on the unicycle.

She rides the unicycle on ice.

She rides the unicycle while
wearing ice skates and playing
the cymbals all at once.

Her talents never cease to amaze the audience. Tonight, as Celia is about to go on stage,

she notices her parents.
"**Come** home, Celia," they say.

THE AMAZING
CELIA!

Celia runs onto the stage and
performs better than ever.

She skates, cycles, and clashes
her cymbals. She is fantastic.

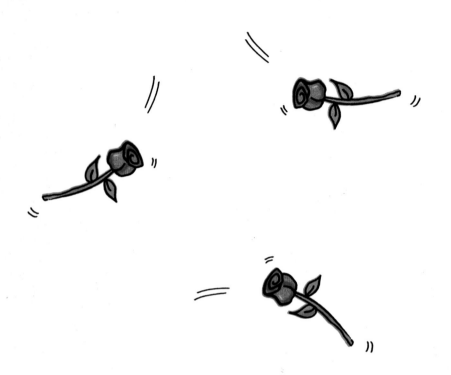

"Hurray!" everyone shouts.

"Amazing!" cheer Celia's parents.
"Let's celebrate. You can stay on
the stage, as long as you get home
in time to do your homework."

Celia agrees.

One day Celia might want
to be a celebrity physicist.

OVER 48 TITLES IN SIX LEVELS
Betty Franchi recommends...

Some titles from Level 4

I love reading phonics — The Circus Mice — 978 1 84898 783 8

I love reading phonics — Monster's Night — 978 1 84898 784 5

I love reading phonics — Jemima The Spy — 978 1 84898 785 2

Other titles to enjoy from Level 5

I love reading phonics — The Gigantic Bear — 978 1 84898 787 6

I love reading phonics — The Cemetery Dance — 978 1 84898 789 0

I love reading phonics — Goose Flight — 978 1 84898 790 6

Some titles from Level 6

I love reading phonics — Hugh is New — 978 1 84898 791 3

I love reading phonics — Clumsy Eagle — 978 1 84898 792 0

I love reading phonics — Bad Zombie Movie — 978 1 84898 793 7

An Hachette Company
First published in the United States by TickTock, an imprint of Octopus Publishing Group.
www.octopusbooksusa.com

Copyright © Octopus Publishing Group Ltd 2013

Distributed in the US by
Hachette Book Group USA
237 Park Avenue, New York NY 10017, USA

Distributed in Canada by
Canadian Manda Group
165 Dufferin Street, Toronto, Ontario, Canada M6K 3H6

ISBN 978 1 84898 788 3

Printed and bound in China
10 9 8 7 6 5 4 3 2 1

CELIA'S PROFESSOR PARENTS WANT HER TO BE A PHYSICIST, BUT SHE IS DETERMINED TO BE A CELEBRITY.

I love reading phonics is a new reading series, offering beginner readers a structured literacy program that combines fun illustrated fiction with phonics learning.

Series consultant Betty Franchi says:

"I love reading phonics is a unique and fun way to introduce emergent readers to the joy of reading and to stimulate beginning readers to improve their reading skills."

Betty Franchi is an American educator qualified in Elementary, Middle and Special Education. She has proven expertise in Phonetic Awareness and the implementation of phonetic strategies.

CELEBRITY CELIA LEVEL 5 BOOK F

LEVEL 1 – All 26 alphabet sounds and pairs of letters representing one alphabet sound

LEVEL 2 – Pairs of letters representing consonant sounds

LEVEL 3 – Pairs and groups of letters representing vowel sounds

LEVEL 4 – Alternative spellings of consonant sounds

LEVEL 5
- focuses on alternative spellings of consonant sounds e.g. g/ge/dge
- includes shorter and longer words containing alternative spellings of consonant sounds e.g. gym/barge/hedge

LEVEL 6 – Letters that represent more than one sound

Next title in the series: *The Cemetery Dance*

ISBN 978-1-84898-788-3

9 781848 987883

US $3.99   Canada $4.50
www.octopusbooksusa.com

Tick
Tock

Hugh
is New